Black Belt

Matt Faulkner

ALFRED A. KNOPF
New York

I would like to dedicate *Black Belt* to the many friends and members of my family who helped in its creation.

"Karate ni sente nashi."
("There is no first strike in karate.")

THIS IS A BORZOI BOOK PUBLISHED BY
ALFRED A. KNOPF

Copyright © 2000 by Matt Faulkner
All rights reserved under International
and Pan-American Copyright Conventions.
Published in the United States of America
by Alfred A. Knopf, a division of Random
House, Inc., New York, and simultaneously
in Canada by Random House of Canada
Limited, Toronto. Distributed by Random
House, Inc., New York.

KNOPF, BORZOI BOOKS, and the colophon are
registered trademarks of Random House, Inc.

www.randomhouse.com/kids

Library of Congress
Cataloging-in-Publication Data
Faulkner, Matt.
Black belt / Matt Faulkner.
p.   cm.
Summary: After hiding in a karate school
to escape a bully, Bushi wakes up in another
time and learns from a karate master that
intelligence can be more powerful than
mere strength.
ISBN 0-375-80157-X (trade)
ISBN 0-375-90157-4 (lib. bdg.)
[1. Karate—Fiction. 2. Bullies—Fiction.
3. Japan—Fiction.] I. Title.
PZ7.F2765   B12000
[E]—dc21   99-88442

May 2000
Printed in Singapore
10 9 8 7 6 5 4 3 2 1

The meanings of the Japanese names and words used in the story:

bushi: little warrior

dojo: school or practice hall for the martial arts

karate do: the way of the empty hand

oji: uncle

samurai: warrior

taka: hawk

yag-yu: the wild one

zuki: punch

My name is Bushi. In my school, all the little kids were called Guppies. The big kids called themselves Bullfrogs. They thought they were cool in their black uniforms and sunglasses. After school, the Bullfrogs would hang around by the front gate, waiting to pick on Guppies. I was a Guppy.

One day, a tough Bullfrog named Yag-yu grabbed me by the arm.

"Hey, Guppy," said Yag-yu. "When are you gonna comb that hair?" He laughed as he started to pour soda on my head.

"No!" I yelled. I was tired of being picked on. I spun around and waved my arms. Somehow, I knocked the soda can out of Yag-yu's hand. It flew through the air and spilled all over his school uniform.

Yag-yu looked very angry. He tried to grab me, but I was too fast for him. I started running. Yag-yu and the Bullfrogs were right behind me. I ran as fast as I could. But I couldn't get away from them.

I turned a corner. I was too tired to run any farther. Nearby, there was a door. I turned the handle and stepped inside, just in time. I could hear the Bullfrogs as they ran past the door and down the street. For the moment, I was safe.

I climbed a flight of stairs and found myself in a karate school. A black belt hanging on the wall caught my eye. A sign below it read THIS BELT BELONGED TO THE MASTER. HE WAS A SMALL MAN WITH A BIG HEART AND THE SPIRIT OF A TIGER.

I thought: *If I had the spirit of a tiger, I'd show those Bullfrogs.* I took the belt down from the wall and tied it around my waist. Then I heard someone coming up the stairs. I tried to run, but my foot got tangled in the belt. I tripped and fell. When my head hit the floor, everything went black.

When I woke, there was a real samurai sitting next to me. He was huge. He shook me a few times. "Bushi, wake up."

I closed my eyes. When I opened them again, he was still there. I sat up. "Who are you?" I said.

The samurai became very excited. "Bushi! It's me—your best friend, Zuki!" He picked me up. "Help!" he cried. "Taka, where are you?"

Just then, another samurai appeared. He smiled at me. "Hello, Bushi," he said. "Did you have a nice trip?"

"Taka," said Zuki, "I knocked Bushi down. Now his brain is rattled."

Taka put his hand on my head. "He has a small bump," he said. "But I think he will be fine. Come on, let's sit in the garden."

We sat in a beautiful garden. All around us, people were practicing karate. It was very quiet, even peaceful. Someone rang a bell.

"Class is over," said Taka. "Let's go hear what the Master has to say."

The Master stood before his students. "You have practiced well today," he said. "I am proud of you. But before you leave, I must warn you: terrible danger waits for you in the hills.

"A most horrible bandit has been attacking villagers up on the mountain paths. No one has been able to withstand the brute. I am told he is a fearsome fighter. Please be careful on your way home tonight."

Zuki jumped to his feet. "Master, I am not afraid!"

The students gave a loud cheer, but the Master raised his hand and they quickly fell silent.

"Zuki, I have no doubt you are brave, but it is your head and not your heart that must guide you tonight. If you meet this bandit on the road, turn and walk the other way."

"Bushi," said Taka, "it's too dangerous for you to walk home alone."

"Yes," said Zuki. "Tonight you come with us." We bowed to the Master and started up the mountain path.

High up on the mountain, we heard laughter. A wild man was dancing in the moonlight. "This is my path!" he yelled. "No one shall pass!"

Zuki shook his fist at the bandit. "You don't frighten me!" he shouted.

The bandit laughed. "Run along home, boy, or you'll pay the price!"

Zuki was furious. He raced up the hill, swinging his fists. Back and forth he chased the bandit, but he just couldn't seem to hit him. Finally, he became exhausted. He swayed back and forth, gulping for air. The bandit was on him in a flash. With one or two lightning-fast strikes, he knocked Zuki to the ground.

Taka put his hand on my shoulder. "Bushi, run back to the garden and get the Master! Hurry!" I started to run, but stopped when I came to Zuki, lying in the path. I helped him to sit up.

"Thank you," he said. "I will be all right in a moment."

Up on the hill, Taka faced the bandit alone.

"Come here, boy!" cried the bandit. "I will teach you a lesson you won't soon forget!"

"No, thank you," replied Taka. "But you may come and get me if you dare."

The bandit howled with rage and charged at Taka. Taka stood his ground.

Everything happened very quickly. One moment, Taka was standing in the path, waiting patiently for the bandit. The next moment, he was riding on the bandit's back. The bandit lost his balance, tripped, and landed with a thud. Taka jumped up, tore the belt from the bandit's waist, and tied his hands and feet.

"Well done," said Zuki when Taka sat down beside us.

"Thank you," said Taka. "But it was a close call. Luckily, I remembered one of the Master's favorite sayings: 'It is always best to get out of the way of a charging bull.'"

When Zuki was feeling better, the three of us carried the bandit back to the Master's garden. Taka knocked on the Master's gate. No one answered. "Master, where are you?" yelled Zuki.

"I'm right behind you."

We turned to see the bandit standing there, his hands and feet untied.

He reached up and pulled the wig from his head and the patch from his eye. "Dear students," he said, "it is only I, your teacher. Please forgive me this prank I have played on you tonight."

"Come inside," said the Master. "We will have some tea and talk about tonight's adventures.

"Zuki, of all my students you are the strongest and the bravest. But you must learn to think before you strike. It might save you a few headaches."

Zuki bowed. "Thank you, Master."

"Taka, jumping onto my back was a marvelous idea. You caught me completely by surprise. However, your knot tying does require some practice."

Taka bowed. "Thank you, Master."

The Master turned to me. "Bushi, you showed great courage by staying with your friends in the face of such danger. You truly have the spirit of a tiger." I stood up and bowed to the Master.

"Ho ho!" the Master cried. "Bushi, you've found my favorite belt." He pointed at the black belt around my waist. "May I have it back now?"

I untied the knot in the Master's belt. When I took a step forward, my foot got tangled in the belt and I tripped. It seemed as if I might never stop falling.

I woke up and found myself back in the karate school. A man was sitting next to me. "Hello," he said. "My name is Mr. Oji. This is my dojo. There were some tough guys outside looking for someone named Bushi. Would that be you?"

"Yes," I replied. "They are angry with me."

"Hmmm. Perhaps you shouldn't leave just yet," said Mr. Oji. "Class will begin soon, Bushi. You may join us if you wish."

"Thank you." I took off the black belt and hung it on the wall. "I'm sorry I tried on the Master's belt," I said.

"No harm done," said Mr. Oji.

Soon, the room was filled with karate students. We did lots of exercises and plenty of stretching. Then I learned how to block a punch. Mr. Oji told me that I was very good for a beginner. "Come back tomorrow," he said, "and I'll show you how to perform the Master's favorite kick."

After class, Mr. Oji walked home with me. I introduced him to my mom. Mr. Oji invited me to join his dojo. My mom thought it was a wonderful idea. I did too.

The next day, I couldn't wait for school to end. When the bell finally rang, I ran out the front gate— straight into the Bullfrogs! I was trapped. "You're not getting away this time, Guppy!" said Yag-yu.

"You're going to pay for messing up my best school uniform!" shouted Yag-yu. Then he ran straight at me. I was really scared! I wanted to cry, but at the last moment I remembered the Master's favorite saying: "It is always best to get out of the way of a charging bull."

Just as Yag-yu was about to run over me, I stepped to one side and jumped onto his back.

Yag-yu took a few wobbly steps, then tripped. We fell into the frog pond. For a second, everything was quiet. Yag-yu looked at me.

The rest of the Bullfrogs rushed up to the pond. I thought I was in for it, but they didn't pay any attention to me. They started to make fun of Yag-yu. I climbed out of the pond.

As I crossed the street, I hoped that would be the last I'd see of Yag-yu. I decided not to think about Yag-yu and the Bullfrogs. Instead, I thought about Zuki, Taka, and the Master. Maybe the Master was right. Maybe I do have the spirit of a tiger.

I started to walk a little faster. I didn't want to be late for Mr. Oji's karate class.